Time for a Break
Short Stories

A Collection of Romance, Mystery,
& Apocalyptic Adventure

D1714545

Jackie Zack

ISBN: 9798858754848

Dedicated to all of us who need a break. ☺

CONTENTS

ACKNOWLEDGMENTS

Thank you to my wonderful family, friends, and ACFW
scribes group. All of you are the best.
Very special thanks to Sally Johns
and Sue Diefenbach.

.

Romance

Enchanted Spring

Kyla picked up her pink sweater and stared as it slipped through her fingertips. How conflicted she was. Her go-to sweater which seemed to be the epitome of her essence, light-hearted and carefree, now held memories of her ex. She glanced at the cardboard containers around her apartment. How would she know what to keep? She needed clothing and household items, but bad memories tainted them.

Why had she stayed with him for so long? The question would haunt her for years. True, she'd wanted the marriage to work. But why hadn't she seen his manipulative nature? Why had she doubted herself?

She sighed. Single again at thirty-three.

Her phone rang. Mom again. *What now?*

"Hello?" Kyla's voice sounded tired even to her

own ears.

"I need a quick favor."

"I'm right in the middle of unpacking." Almost the truth. She'd just started, but it had taken a couple of hours to psych herself up for the task.

"Well, you need a break."

Kyla stood and rested a hand on a stack of boxes. A break that consisted of another tedious assignment, no doubt.

"I've made an appointment with a dog walker."

"Dog walker? You don't have a dog." She paused. "Did you get a dog?"

"No, no." Her mother laughed. "I mean, I have an appointment with the people walker."

"What?" Kyla squinted her eyes and pressed fingers to the middle of her forehead. "People walker?"

"Yes, a sweetheart of a man…"

Right. Was it even possible for a man to be sweet?

"He's a man in my apartment building. He's put together a walking service for us older folks."

"So, what's the favor?"

"I can't keep the appointment." Her mother's voice held disappointment. "I need you to take my place."

"Can't you call it off? Reschedule?"

"I've already paid through PayPal and don't want the money to go to waste."

"Why can't you go?"

"Something came up with Helen."

"Oh." Something always came up with Aunt Helen. Unexpected shopping needs, troubles with her runaway cat, and cooking mishaps.

"You'll enjoy it. All the flowering trees are in bloom. Plus, you can relax. No worries about strangers bothering you with him around. He's an ex-cop. A widower."

Kyla's gaze dropped to the box of clothing. *Good grief.* Walk around town with some old guy? How did she get stuck in these predicaments?

Her mom continued, "My friend Deloris highly recommends him."

Oh, yes. "Deloris highly recommends a lot of things." Actually, everything. Kyla could tell her mother no, but Mom wanted her to enjoy the flowers, the experience. Kyla glanced out the window. It kind of sounded like an adventure. A quirky one at that. "What time?"

She picked up her pink sweater.

****

When would his next appointment arrive? Liam glanced at his watch as he waited by the apartment building's entrance. Ornamental pear trees bloomed along the city sidewalks. A nearby bed of red tulips competed with a section of yellow.

A sweet flower-scented breeze wafted by.

He turned and focused upward at the four-story building. Which floor did she live on? Hopefully, she'd be able to walk okay. So far, most of his clients did well.

His idea of being a people walker had been a godsend for the seniors and himself. He'd gotten to know his clients and considered them friends if not family. They'd each received great exercise and conversation at the same time. He loved having the activity after work and on weekends. A Band-Aid for his emotions.

The time with the newly retired Miss Deloris came to mind. She loved to tease and said he looked like John Wick. He'd laughed and asked if she meant from the movies or the books. She'd looked over her glasses at him and said, *"Why, the movies, of course. Except you're younger. How old are you? Thirty?"*

He'd answered that he was an old thirty-six.

She'd waved away his words, then shook her head. *"That's not old."*

At thirty, he'd married the love of his life. Thank God, they'd at least had five years.

Minutes ticked by. An attractive woman about his age strolled up the sidewalk to the apartment building. Lovely brown hair draped over the shoulders of her pink sweater. Dark lashes accentuated blue eyes. Her perfect lips were a coral pink. When her eyes locked with his and she slightly smiled, he lost his breath. How enchanting.

She stood two paces away from him and faced the street as he did.

Long seconds ticked by.

"Waiting for someone?" he asked.

"Yes." She nodded.

"Me too."

****

Kyla couldn't get over the handsome man who stood about six feet to her left. If only he were the son of the dog walker. Oops! People walker.

Wow. She'd love to get to know him, but her skills at conversing with the opposite sex had taken a blow. Her confidence ebbed near zero due to all the putdowns from her ex.

Would other men have some of the same thoughts about her? She hoped not.

She stole another glance at the man. And again, all she could think was wow. Tall. Strong build. Dark hair, including neatly-trimmed beard and mustache. He had a calm peace about him. His brown eyes held compassion.

She chided herself. Someone that good-looking must be married or, at least, have a girlfriend. *Calm down.*

"It looks like Tanya isn't coming," he said.

Kyla's eyes popped. *What?* That was her

mother's name. Her legs turned weak. "Did you say, Tanya?"

"Yes, that's right."

"You…you're the dog walker—I mean—people walker?"

"I am." He half-smiled.

"Tanya's my mother. I'm here to take her place."

His eyes widened, and he took in a surprised breath. "Really? Excellent. Let's go."

Handsome dimples appeared as he smiled, and she couldn't help but smile in return.

Romance Follows

Rafe Sinclair stood by a jewelry shop and peered in the window. He'd found information online that pearl was the designated gift for a thirtieth anniversary. They'd celebrate it next month. What would his darling Patty like? She hovered by his elbow and no doubt saw the earrings, bangles, and necklaces sparkling in the sun. How fun to purchase an anniversary gift for her while they vacationed at Treasure Island. How could he keep it a surprise?

He turned ever so slightly to get a glimpse of her to ascertain what she might be admiring. She'd vanished. Prickles zinged down his neck. Good grief! How could he lose his wife so quickly?

He looked down the sidewalk to his left and then to the right. No sign of her at all. He studied the people across the street. Not there either. He tamped down rising anxiety and reached for his phone in a back pocket. He drew in a sharp breath. Gone. He must've left it in the hotel room.

He hated to admit he felt like a lost boy at a supermarket.

Tourists ambled by with the scent of coconut suntan lotion. Palm branches fluttered in the breeze. Everything was at peace and yet, not.

His fingers pressed against the graying whiskers of his chin, then raked through his equally graying hair. Well, the first rule of being lost was that one must stay in place and not wander aimlessly. But his dear wife was lost, not him...right? Still, he planted his feet in place and eyed the surrounding area for any trace of his dark-haired beauty.

Earlier that morning, he'd asked if she might like to return to her natural blonde. A faraway look in her eye told him she considered his words and also indicated some sort of plan or surprise. She loved to tease him.

Hmm. Were there any beauty parlors nearby? He could well imagine her laughter as she slipped away to a walk-in salon. She'd return hours later as a blonde and say something like, oh, there you are. In spite of everything, he chuckled inside.

Wig shops! Were there any? He glanced over the stores again. Nope. Any other shop she might like? He sighed. Could be any of them.

He turned around, gazed inside the jewelry shop, and locked on the profile of a familiar woman in a pink dress. She smiled and resumed perusing items in a display case.

Ha, ha. Gotcha. She'd no doubt seen his meltdown on the sidewalk.

He strode to the entrance and stepped inside. A bell announced his arrival with a *ding-dong*. Display cases in a variety of shapes and styles sat on dark-teal carpet. Light blue-gray walls added to the cool ambiance. He sidled up to the dark-haired beauty and scrutinized the rings in the case.

What? Wedding sets? Had she lost her fondness for the ring he had made for her from his grandmother's diamond?

"Honey. Engagement rings?"

The woman stepped away from him to look at another grouping.

He followed her. "You'd like a ring?"

"It's what I'm looking for."

Uh-oh. Not Patty's voice. His eyes shot to the woman's face. "Sorry, I thought you were my wife."

The woman's eyebrows lifted. "Oh?"

"Sorry," he repeated and put more distance between them. Yes, hard to believe since she appeared twenty years younger than he and Patty. How embarrassing.

And it meant Patty was still missing. He returned to the sidewalk and stood like a mournful puppy.

****

Patty picked up a candle decorated with shells. Rafe had followed her, hadn't he? Or he'd at least seen her step into the collectibles shop. She pulled out her phone and texted: *Where are you? I'm at Sally's Seashells.*

She held her phone, expecting a return message, and moved to the soap section. A light lavender scent wafted through the air. She took in a breath and relaxed. Rafe was obviously preoccupied. She slipped her phone into her purse and made her way through the aisles with a candle and a bar of soap.

She peered around each corner. Colorful beach towels, flip flops, and sunglasses tempted her as well as beach-themed household decorations, but no Rafe in sight. Her mind's eye supplied her a picture of him in his new Hawaiian shirt in blues and greens. His heartbreaking smile and the softness of his brown eyes made her heart tug as he regarded her new outfit.

Patty smiled and looked down at her pink retro culottes dress. She'd found an old pattern and had sewn it herself. A sudden urge to fall into his arms and breathe in his masculine cologne overwhelmed her. She set her items by the cash register and told the clerk she'd be right back. Once outside, she looked up and down the sidewalk past the meandering tourists, her hand shielding her eyes from the bright sun.

Had he stopped at the jeweler's? She placed a hand on her hip. He was probably trying to be sneaky and find her some kind of surprise. What a dear heart. Well, he knew where to find her since she'd sent a text.

She returned to Sally's Seashells. Maybe she could find a gift for him.

****

Rafe glanced at his watch. How much time had gone by? He had no idea. The Patty look-alike stepped out of the jewelry shop. He intentionally looked the other way and stood by different window.

He wiped a hand over his face. What would their kids think when he called them to say he'd lost their mom? *Calm down, Rafe.* Patty had to backtrack sooner or later.

His eyes focused on a natural pink pearl necklace. Oh, a perfect gift for Patty. He looked up and down the sidewalk once more, then stepped back into the store. He strode toward the counter to get the elderly female clerk's attention. Right at the last second, a distinguished older man with white hair stepped up to her in front of Rafe.

"Can I help you?" she asked with a warbly voice and put on a pair of purple-framed glasses.

The man drummed his fingertips on the glass counter. "I'm looking for a fiftieth wedding anniversary gift."

"For?"

"My wife of course."

"Okay, you'll want diamonds and gold."

"Well, yes."

Rafe started to sweat. How long would this take? He started to head back outside as two women pointed to the pink pearl necklace. No! It was the only one as far as he could tell. At least he stood next in line. Since it was part of the display, they couldn't reach it and buy it before he did.

"Would you like a bracelet? Earrings? Necklace? Or a ring?" the clerk asked.

"Good question," the white-haired man said.

"I'd go with earrings." Rafe gave a smile and a nod.

The older man turned toward him. "Why?"

"Because they would be closer to your wife's lovely face."

"I like the way you think, young man."

Young man? A man of fifty, young?

Minute after long minute passed. The older man decided on a pair of stylish earrings dripping with diamonds.

"Good choice," Rafe said sincerely.

The white-haired gentleman smiled, dipped his head, and hummed as he walked out of the store, still wearing the pleased smile.

Rafe nearly tripped trying to step up to the clerk.

"I'd like to purchase the natural pink pearl necklace in the window."

She stared at him with wide eyes. What could be wrong now?

"It's a thirty-year anniversary gift. For my wife."

"Very nice." She smiled.

Rafe blew out a breath. He looked at his watch. He still didn't know how long he'd been lost from Patty, but twenty more minutes had gone by.

"They are fresh-water pearls. That's what gives them their pink color." The clerk adjusted her glasses.

"Ah. Interesting."

"Let me get the key for the window display." The lady leaned down to a cabinet. "Let's see, which drawer has the key?"

Rafe glanced outside to see if Patty might pass by. He continued to sweat. Drawers thumped open and thumped closed. The lady found the key. The necklace was retrieved, paid for, put in a box, and then the box placed in a bag. Each step taking an eternity.

At last, he had the bag in hand. He sighed with relief. "Thank you."

"You're welcome. Come again."

Out of the corner of his eyes, he saw a woman in pink walk toward him. She neared and stood close. "How wonderful. Buying something for your wife? I wish my husband would do that. He just disappeared."

"I had the same problem. One minute my wife stood by my side. And then the next…gone. I'm not sure what to tell our children." He headed toward the door as she walked with him.

"I'll bet she texted you. Several times. Did you even check?" Her green eyes widened.

He touched his back pocket, then shrugged. "Phone's gone."

"Ah. The old missing phone routine."

Rafe's brow furrowed. "Routine? No…no routine. I love my wife very much."

"You do?"

As they reached the door, he put an arm around Patty and pulled her close, squashing her against him. She laughed, then accepted his kiss, a dreamy stolen kiss he never wanted to end.

The door to the jewelry shop opened and a surprised younger couple both said, "Oh!"

Patty broke away from his kiss, lightly pushed his chest, and laughed. "Newlyweds," she explained.

"She's teasing." Rafe smiled and pointed to Patty, then to himself. "Thirty years."

The young woman's hand flew to her heart. "Really?"

"Congratulations, old man," the younger guy said.

Old man? Not quite. Rafe chuckled. "Thanks."

He and Patty stepped out into the sun once more.

Rafe's gaze dropped to the shopping bag Patty held. Inside, a box showed a beach-themed lava lamp. He sighed inwardly. She knew him so well.

Patty, the love of his life.

Year of the Cat

Oliver let the screen door close with a thwack as he strolled to his car. A blurry gray image raced by his feet. Both he and the mouse had bad timing. The rodent clung to the toe of his shoe, then flew through the air with his next stride. What in the world?

He turned to his grandmother who stood inside the door and watched his departure. "Grandma, we have to do something about the mice."

"Don't worry. It's The Year of the Cat, for sure." She opened the screen door, and her light hair fluttered in the breeze. Their cat Tiger slipped outside and meowed.

"It'd better be. The field mice will take over if they can." He paused. "Won't you come with me?"

"No, dear." She waved. "Enjoy the Bogart

movie."

"I will." He waved in return.

Grandma smiled and placed a hand on her cheek as if she knew something he didn't.

His high school class of '76 graduation was now tucked in the past. He'd move soon to an apartment near the state college campus. But he'd make sure to visit.

Minutes later, he settled in an antique seat at the town cinema. Grandma had said she'd actually watched Casablanca here in 1942. *Whoa.*

The room darkened, and the movie started to play. What a different time and place it had been. If only he could slip back into time and visit for a moment.

Half an hour in, his eyelids became heavy. He hadn't gotten much sleep the night before. His brain had let him imagine any and all scenarios about his life. What would college be like? Should he take more time and rethink his career choice of accounting? *Be quiet brain.* It was a good choice.

When the movie came to its drama-filled conclusion, he stepped outside into the bright daylight. An intense light flickered off a car's windshield. The quick flash momentarily hurt his head. He turned away and pinched the bridge of his nose.

As he opened his eyes, a bus by the side of the road caught his attention. Was it part of the old-time theme? The bus driver wore a 1940's-style suit and pointed to a sign with his cane. Roundtrip Excursion to Sadieville.

Oliver crept toward the group purchasing tickets as if he were Peter Lorrie planning a crime. His grandma expected him home sometime that day. He'd get home in the evening, no problem.

Last in line, he purchased the tickets and found a seat on the bus. He'd always wanted to check out Sadieville. The obscure town could be found on a janky journey of unpaved roads. Neighboring burgs other than his hometown of Bellefontaine had an easy paved route. It made no sense.

His friends had talked about Sadieville, but only in short descriptions. They'd end with, *"Well, you'll just have to see it for yourself."* Then they'd laugh. He could never discern if they'd enjoyed it or thought it strange.

As they traveled, he kept a mental note of the county road numbers along with the twisting turns. Why he thought it important he had no idea. Forested areas passed by in between sun-drenched farmland.

After the bus went through a tunnel of trees and greenery, the sky opened up, and they pulled into Sadieville.

Oliver followed the crowd off the bus. Old-time stores and restaurants lined both sides of Main Street. The sun's yellow rays blinded him for a second. He shielded his eyes with a hand on his brow.

A girl with golden wavy hair glowing in the sunshine rushed toward him. Her silky dress flowed with shades of pink that ran together like a watercolor caught in the rain. "Oliver, you came!" She smiled.

She knew his name? What? How? "I'm sorry. Do we know each other?"

The beautiful girl tilted her head. Her smile grew, and she laughed. Before he knew it, she'd captured his arm in hers, and they took off down the street.

"I'm so glad you finally came."

"You've been waiting for me? Do you have me confused with someone else?" He turned to look behind him.

"Oh, you tease. This way. You're going to like Sadieville."

"Do you live here?"

A faraway look appeared in her eyes. "I came in the year of the cat."

"When was that? What does that mean?"

"Hurry, come on, this way." She clasped his hand and didn't give him time for any more questions.

They wound through the crowd to vendor's tables draped in blue. The merchants sold a variety of artwork, books, and crafts. Next, she led him to an alleyway where jewelry, purses, and blankets were sold. His head spun with all the colors and designs. She tugged his hand as the crowd grew denser. When she dashed around a corner, he lost his grip.

Oliver stepped around the building and scanned the sightseers. Where was she? Had he lost her for good?

She popped out from an old brick store entryway, smiled, and waved. Oliver hurried to meet her. She passed a craftsman selling ceramics and motioned to a display of top-quality billfolds in a variety of styles. The earthy scent of leather met his nostrils.

"Aren't they wonderful?" she asked. "I'll bet you could use one."

"Yes, but they're…" The word expensive stalled in his mouth when he locked eyes with the booth owner. The man's deeply lined face appeared as tough as the leather he worked with. "Awesome," Oliver finally said.

A black wallet emblazoned with a running horse fueled his imagination. How wonderful to own such a unique piece.

A fluttering sensation touched his back pocket. He turned. A boy ran off with his wallet.

"He took my wallet!" Oliver dashed after the boy. He could only hope the attractive blonde would follow him.

"Please stop him! He stole my wallet," Oliver exclaimed to the tourists.

Onlookers stared at him and the boy. Oliver dashed down an alleyway full of junk-food trucks to follow the small villain. Then the boy's profile emerged around the corner of an elephant ear stand.

Oliver took steady steps toward him as if he didn't see the boy, then gently grabbed him.

"I think you have something of mine."

The boy's eyes teared. "I'm sorry." He returned the wallet.

"It's wrong to steal," Oliver said.

"I know. I'm sorry. I'm hungry." His brown eyes cast downward.

"How about asking instead of taking?"

The boy took in a breath and nodded. "Please."

Someone gripped Oliver's arm. The nameless girl stood beside him. She smiled sadly.

"Elephant ear?" he asked the boy.

"Yes, please."

"Let's get in line."

Thankfully, not too many waited for the treat since so many food choices were offered.

"I'm Oliver." He pointed to his chest, then glanced at the mysterious blonde.

She bent down to the boy's level. "I'm Erin"

"Ben." The youngster blushed. "I promise I won't ever do it again. My mom started a new job. She gets paid tomorrow."

The words bit to Oliver's core. "Okay if we share one?" he asked Erin.

She pressed her lips together and gave a quick nod.

He used all the money from his wallet and bought three.

As Oliver handed two to Ben, he said, "For you and your mom."

"Thanks, mister," the boy said sincerely and waved. "I won't ever forget it."

Would Ben and his mom be all right? Oliver prayed they would.

He watched as the youngster disappeared into the throngs of people.

As Oliver held the elephant ear, Erin pulled off a piece of their sugary treat. She motioned with a tilt of her head. "This way."

While they ate, they meandered through the rest of the displays in a dizzying pattern of short streets. If only he'd kept track of the names. He had no idea where Main Street was anymore. Not to mention the sequence of county roads had totally left his memory.

Once the treat was gone, they stopped at a fountain to rinse their hands. Then they were off again to another section of town.

"Isn't it beautiful here?" she asked.

"Yes." But it was more than that—surreal, uncanny.

"My life here is refreshing like a river running through a desert." Her eyes reflected that notion. Blue, cool, and calm. Bright like the moon shining on ocean waves.

At a building alcove decorated in indigo tiles, Erin reached to open a small door. Oliver stopped in his tracks. An aroma of incense and patchouli wafted from a nearby store.

"It's okay. It's the back door. I work here."

"What is this place?"

"You'll see. It's The Year of the Cat."

He followed her. His expression must've turned puzzled. She smiled. What waited inside?

She led him to a lobby and purchased drinks and popcorn for them.

"It's a movie theater?" he asked.

"Yes, I thought for sure you'd like it. Do you remember me now? Erin is my middle name."

Oliver studied her lovely face. She did look familiar. "I—"

"It's okay. You'll remember."

They sat comfortably in the dark theater and watched old-time movies, one after the other, laughing and crying together. The hour grew late, but he didn't care. He didn't want to leave.

The next thing he knew, he woke up to see Erin sleeping beside him. The theater—quiet, empty.

"Wake up." He touched her arm.

Her eyes fluttered open.

"I'm afraid it's very late. I should be heading home."

"Oh! Yes."

As they exited the building, the morning sun appeared on the horizon. The bus had left hours ago. All of the tourists were gone. He'd have to catch the next bus, whenever that might be. The music from the shows echoed in his mind and gave the new day a theme song.

He opened his billfold to find the return ticket home. His eyes popped. It was gone! It must've slipped out somewhere.

Erin laid a hand on his forearm. "Your ticket's gone?" She sighed. "I wish you'd never have to leave."

"Well, I'll have to stay now." He gave an embarrassed smile and focused on her.

His vision turned to gray fog. What was happening?

Seconds ticked by.

He took in a breath and opened his eyes. Erin's fingers slipped away from his nose and chin. Her soft hair touched his cheek. She'd just given him mouth-to-mouth resuscitation? Her eyes met his.

"You're awake!" she said.

He lay flat on his back on the sidewalk by the old cinema. "What happened?"

"You stepped out from the movie and the sun blinded you. A car almost hit you as it went by. You fell and hit your head."

Wow. His head did hurt. "How long was I out?"

"A half a minute? I worried you weren't breathing."

Moviegoers formed a circle around him. Concerned looks all around.

"It's okay. I'm all right." He moved to stand. Erin

steadied him.

"I was hoping to find you here but not this way," she said. "Your grandma mentioned you'd be here. Do you remember me?"

"I do, Megan." He smiled at the childhood friend who'd moved away years ago. Even back then he'd loved her.

She dipped her head. "I go by my middle name now."

"Erin," he said.

She smiled. "I'm going to State College in the fall. I'd hoped you were too."

"Yes, I am." He remembered how they'd both loved math. "What are you majoring in?"

"Cats."

"What?"

She laughed and squeezed his arm. "Accounting, you silly."

"Great. Me too." *Wow.* How things had a way of working out.

Even though their adventure wasn't real, he'd always remember Sadieville and the Year of the Cat.

Erin looked at him with her cool blue eyes. Or had it all been real?

A bus passed by with a sign that read: Roundtrip Excursion to Sadieville.

Mystery

The Robinson Mansion

"It's still abandoned. Come on." Nick Hinchman swung a metal detector as he walked. "What a great way to spend a day off."

Was this really a good idea? Katy Russell strode beside her coworker toward a distant gray three-story building. It looked like a haunted house on steroids. A center tower structure sported a fourth-floor lookout. On the left, a bump-out of all three floors contained three windows on each story and on the right, two. Cracked panes in most. Two windows gaped open with no glass at all.

For a vacation day, it still smacked of a reporting assignment. She guessed that's what happened when a career turned into a passion. How nice to see him relaxed in a burgundy t-shirt and jeans instead of his professional attire.

"What style is the mansion?" She gave a fleeting glance at Nick's Ford Fiesta barely visible through a tangle of brush. She didn't like the idea of it being parked so far away.

"Empire. Isn't it amazing? Can you imagine what it must've been like to live there so far away from everything?" He turned, and his blue eyes focused on hers.

As they stepped from the shade into the sun, his blond hair lightened.

"Well, considering its past I'm not sure I'd want to. An accidental death, a body buried in the backyard. The owner of the house who'd felt guilty and hanged himself in the tower. No thanks."

"Katy, it couldn't have happened to you."

"For one thing, if I hit someone with my car, I wouldn't go and bury him."

"That was a bad move for sure. They say the victim haunts the woods. The owner haunts the house."

"Who says that?"

"My old high school friends." He chuckled. "Good times. Plus, there are swollen-headed children ghosts who roam around."

"Where'd they come from?"

"Some institution close by."

"Where?" Katy glanced to her left at the thick overgrowth.

"There wasn't one." He smirked.

She laughed. "You came here often?"

"A couple of times."

"That's all?"

"Oh, we got scared off by this and that. He shrugged. "You'll like the beach too. It's about three-quarters of a mile from here."

Minutes later, they made their way to the porch and gazed in. She took in the ancient cream wallpaper with pink and green floral designs, the threadbare carpet, and the old castoff furniture.

"What a sad forgotten place. No one wanted it?" Katy asked.

"Guess not." Nick placed a hand on his hip. "The heir of the place, a grandson, is said to have taken all his inheritance money from the bank and moved to South America."

"That's odd. Who owns the property?"

"Don't know. The county, maybe."

"We shouldn't be here, should we?"

Nick waved away her words. "If a tree falls in a forest and no one hears it…"

"If you go on an excursion with someone who can't see the forest 'cause of the trees…" she teased.

He laughed. "You win, Russell. Want to go back now?"

"Uh, no."

He tried the door. "Locked."

They stepped off the porch and gazed up at the formidable structure. Katy squinted her eyes against the sun and tried to focus on one of the windows missing glass. Only a black gaping hole with no indication of what lay inside.

A gust of wind pushed against them as if to hurry them on their way. She brushed back her long dark hair away from her face.

They circled the house. Nick tried the back door. Locked. All the windows on the first floor remained intact with no way to open them.

"Bummer." He stood and studied the back door.

"Did you see the inside of the house in high school?"

"No. But I'd hoped we would get a look today." He took a step toward the back door and grabbed the doorknob again. "Shoot."

"You're not thinking about breaking in, I hope."

"Of course it crossed my mind, but no."

"Who all knows about this place? It's so far away from the beaten path."

"The legends about the mansion were known, but not its location. My dad accidentally told me. He immediately regretted saying anything about it when he saw my interest. He warned me not to talk about it."

"And you told your friends."

"Yes, but in my defense I swore them to secrecy."

"And you and your friends checked it out?"

Nick nodded.

"So what scared you away?"

"Come on, let's go to the beach." He turned away from the house and breezed past her.

Katy jogged a few paces to catch up. "What? You're not going to tell me?"

His free hand swiped the back of his neck. "You'll think I'm nuts."

"How could I?" Katy hoped her words were true.

He continued at an even pace with a long stride. She hurried to keep up with him. When they neared a rocky path through a forested area, she reached out and tugged his arm. "Nick."

He stopped and turned toward her. His eyes wouldn't meet hers. "I've been over it so many times. I really did see them."

"What?"

He locked eyes with hers. "The swollen-headed kids."

"You actually saw them?" She gasped. "But…"

"I know. It's impossible. But there it is."

"Did your friends see them?"

"No."

"Oh…"

"See what I mean? It's crazy."

"Could it have been something that looked like children?"

He shook his head. "No. They were there one minute and gone the next."

"Hmm. Were they real children?"

"Couldn't be. And it wasn't my imagination."

"Huh. There must be an explanation somewhere."

He blew out a breath. "Thanks. It's been rough not being able to tell anyone."

"You didn't even tell your friends?"

"Are you kidding? No. I wouldn't have heard the end of it."

"Should we come back tonight and see if we can get another sighting?"

"You'd do that?" He half-smiled.

"Why not?"

Nick tilted his head as if he didn't know what to say, then continued down the uneven path.

"Shouldn't you turn on the metal detector?" she asked. After all, wasn't that the main reason for the trip? To try out a new toy.

"Right." He pressed a switch. "For the record, I'm not hoping to find anything, but if we do…"

"What might you find?"

"Old coins. Relics. A lost ring."

"A ring?"

"One of the times we came out, I lost my class ring. Not that I'll find it. But it won't hurt to try. It's weird to think of it being outside and in the dirt for this long."

Katy almost teased that an offspring from one of the misshapen kids probably had it, but decided against it. The sighting had really rattled him.

33

When the path opened to the beach, the sound of crashing waves competed with the buzz of the metal detector.

"Whoa." Nick's eyes brightened. "Wonder what's there." He turned off the detector, then gazed at the beach. "Boy, there's been a lot of erosion. The beach has shrunk to half the size."

"Still a nice beach." Katy glanced down the coastline to where it stopped at a rocky cliff. Several seagulls drifted on the wind. One of them cried.

He pulled a trowel from a back pocket and started digging. The soil was sandy, so it was just a matter of scooping it up and moving it out of the way.

After he reached about ten inches down, she asked, "How much farther do you think?"

"The detector can read a metal object about 16 inches down." Just as he said the last word, the trowel hit something. He brushed the soil away with his hands. "It looks like a handle."

"A handle?"

He frowned. "A knife handle."

"Be careful."

"Yes, ma'am." He winked.

He pushed the sandy soil away, making the hole wider and deeper. The dark handle stood upright in the sand. The blade appeared to be plunged into something. Then she caught a glimpse of plaid material.

"Oh. Uh-oh." Nick rocked back onto his heels

and stood.

"Is that..?" She didn't want to say it.

"I think so." He squatted down again and continued to widen the hole.

Moments passed. A head with short red hair appeared. She fought nausea and tried to glance away, yet she couldn't. The man must've been there a very long time. A wrapper protruded from the shirt pocket. With the trowel, Nick eased it out partway. Lucky Strike cigarettes.

Nick glanced up at her, his expression grim.

"Nothing lucky about it," she said.

"You've got that right." He stood and wiped his hands on his pants legs. "I bet the grave started out much deeper and erosion took it away over the years."

He pulled his phone from a pocket. "Shoot. There's no service."

Katy glanced at the makeshift grave. "Maybe that's why the grandson took off to South America."

"To avoid a murder charge?"

She nodded.

"That'd be a good enough reason," he said.

They headed back toward the house. How far would they need to backtrack to get a signal?

About ten minutes later, they neared the mansion which seemed to crackle and sigh in the hot sun.

Nick pulled out his phone. "Nothing." He turned off the metal detector and set it on the ground. "I'm going to try the back door again."

"Okay. I guess the fellow by the beach isn't in a hurry."

Nick flinched at her comment, then jogged to the door. She followed at a leisurely pace. He mumbled something excitedly and motioned.

"What?" she asked.

"The door opened!"

She hurried toward him. The door swung inward. She couldn't believe her eyes. "Did you break the lock?"

"No. The door hasn't weathered well. It must've been jammed in place."

"Wow. Think it's safe to go in?"

"Probably not."

They stepped inside and made their way through the kitchen. Surprisingly enough, it appeared tidy. Katy turned on the water faucet and water gushed out. Her eyes popped. "How can that be?"

"The water was never turned off?"

"But the pipes would've burst in the winter."

Nick opened the refrigerator and a light blinked on. "What? This place can't be abandoned."

"Look, a space heater."

He gazed at it. "Strange."

Nervousness made her tremble inside. "We shouldn't be here."

"Everything else proves it's abandoned. Let's just do a quick check, then leave."

Katy agreed against her better judgment. They crept into the living room. On impulse, she opened the drawers of an old desk. Odds and ends occupied the space, but one drawer held a framed family picture. "Oh, no. Is this the grandson?" The back of her head prickled. The photo showed a handsome young man with red hair.

Nick winced. "That means…"

"Someone killed the grandson? That puts a new spin on things."

"It does."

They continued the search and headed up the stairs, each step creaking loudly. In spite of everything, she loved the old features of the home. But what amount would it take to update the place? It'd have to cost a fortune.

"What do you think? Ready to move in?" Nick smiled.

"It's an amazing place. Lots of room."

"For sure."

They reached the top floor and glanced up at the tower overlook.

"I'm not sure how structurally sound it is up there," Nick said. "So I'll just go."

She made a move to grab his arm but missed.

After a few seconds, he returned. "You've got to see this."

She complied and climbed the steps. The first thing she saw was the lake in the distance, sparkling in the sun. Then she turned, seeing a variety of tree tops over the hilly landscape. "It's beautiful."

"Sure is." He placed his hands on his hips as he took in the sight.

After a moment, they worked their way down and breezed past empty room after empty room, each wall decorated in antique wallpaper. One room made them stop. A wooden box the size and shape of one of the windows clung to an outer wall.

"How strange," Katy exclaimed.

"Yeah." Nick rubbed his chin. "Good grief. It's a cover for one of the windows. The one that didn't have any glass. From the outside, it just looks like a black hole. Know what I mean?"

"Yes. It must be intentional. To give the impression of the house being abandoned." A shiver ran down her spine. "There's probably another one. Next floor down."

"Let's check it out."

Sure enough, the other gaping window had the same treatment. How ingenious. "So someone was or is living here on the sly. You don't think they're still here?"

"I think we'd have met them by now," he said.

"Are you sure about that?"

"No." He shook his head.

Katy took in a breath. She reminded herself again that she and Nick shouldn't be in the mansion. But then again, neither should the squatter. She let out a breath in a whoosh.

"Come on." Nick half smiled. He grabbed her hand to take her out of the room. "This place has character. If I had enough money…"

"But you don't."

He gave her a wide-eyed expression with a hint of a smile.

"Plus, it's too far from work," she added.

"Right."

They headed down the steps which gave off another alarm of creeks and pops.

She and Nick stepped into the kitchen once more.

He opened a door. "Well, there's one last place."

"The basement." She shuddered.

"Ready? Whew, smells rotten. A dead animal?"

She gagged at the rancid odor. Light from the kitchen window illuminated the steps to the depth below. Nick took the lead. As he stepped on the basement floor and turned to round the corner, he jerked to a stop and made a stifled exclamation.

He took in a breath, then said, "Shoot! Well, there you go." He pointed to ominous shapes. Goosebumps zinged on her forearms. Oversized doll heads sat atop child-sized manikins. Five of them altogether. Their glassy eyes glowed in the dim light.

"So that's what you saw! Look, they are on a rack-like device."

Nick touched a corner of the wooden frame, and it moved. The manikins could stand or lay flat.

"A deliberate scare tactic or a prank," she said.

"It worked." He chuckled. "Plus, it started a good round of stories. I wonder who came up with it, the grandson or the murderer."

"Good question."

Nick opened a door to a closed-off room.

Another shock met their eyes. The reason for the smell—right in front of them. A dead older man slumped in an easy chair which faced a flat-screen television. A microwave dinner box lay on the floor along with a can of opened baked beans. The ramshackle room contained a mini-fridge along with a microwave. Stacks and stacks of DVDs littered the room along with empty whiskey bottles.

Were they looking at the one who murdered and buried the Robinson heir? Katy caught a glimpse of an unopened pack of Lucky Strike cigarettes, a wristwatch, and a wallet, all lined up on a shelf underneath a grimy basement window. She'd bet anything the items belonged to the murder victim.

Next to a rickety table sat a duffle bag filled with money. The grandson's inheritance. A theory formed. The man in the chair had, decades ago, coerced the heir to take out all his money from the bank, then killed him. He'd taken over the abandoned house as a hide-out. How had he rigged the water line and electricity? What poor souls were paying the additional amount?

A sick feeling washed over her as she glanced

again at the dead man. He must've died of natural causes.

Katy left the room.

Nick followed her. They headed up the stairs and strode out of the house. He closed the door with much effort.

"Wow. There's gotta be a good article in this," Nick said.

"Hinchman, it's supposed to be our day off!" Katy crossed her arms. Not to mention the upset over finding two dead bodies.

She wanted to give him grief, but at every level, she understood and outright loved his enthusiasm. Digging up and getting at the truth. That's what he lived for.

"After the cops get here and we give our statements, let's grab some lunch," he said.

"Along with pie?"

"You know it."

Katy focused on the metal detector. They hadn't found Nick's ring. No doubt they'd return again someday. She put a hand to her brow as she gazed at the unkempt grounds. Hopefully, Robinson Mansion had nothing else to hide.

The Rondel Dagger

I'd been the *lucky* one out of twenty applicants. The private investigator's chosen candidate for the personal assistant job. I glanced at the lone decoration on the beige walls, my calendar. Now this month, lucky for two years.

The phone rang and broke the silence. As I picked it up, my boss said, "Sandi, get that."

I widened my eyes and wagged the receiver at him. I had it in my hand. *The nerve.* "Office of Jack Hackathorn, PI. How may I help you?"

"Put Jack on the phone," Mira screeched. "It's *so* like him not to answer his cell phone." My boss's redhead girlfriend killed my ear. *Drat.* If two narcissistic people could win a prize for a perfect match, they'd get first place. Critical, selfish, and the list went on.

"It's Mira." I offered him the receiver.

Jack's face turned an unhealthy shade of red. "Take a message."

"Don't you dare take a message," Mira trilled loud enough this time for it to reach my boss's ears.

He raked a hand through salt and pepper hair, snatched the phone, and turned his back on me. "What do you want? We're trying to juggle three important cases."

I rolled my eyes. Not true.

"You *must* come right away. They say Mr. Yetter's been killed." her voice blared into the room.

My stomach lurched at the words. Prickles covered my face. Our phone call from two days ago came to mind. Had he told the police his suspicions?

"I'll be right there." Jack slammed the phone down and grabbed his coat.

As I opened a metal drawer to retrieve my purse, he turned and glared. "You can't go."

"He's my uncle."

My boss cleared his throat. "Come along then."

****

When Jack flashed his PI license, we obtained clearance to enter the Yetter Manor. I couldn't believe my uncle's body lay lifeless in his home office. We and the staff were barred from the room and milled about in the outer lobby where my uncle kept his medieval collection. I dropped onto a chair near the front door. Scenes from different ages of my life flashed before my eyes along with snippets of conversation. He loved to tell me about the various weapons.

Uncle Drew had always brightened when he'd secured a new piece. With no wife or children to tend to, the hobby consumed him. I gazed at the collection. Double-sided axes, fantastic swords, a ball and chain flail with a suit of armor, and a large variety of daggers. It gave an ambiance to the room for sure, but I couldn't discern what kind. Gothic protection?

He'd always said he wanted to live in medieval times. And what better way to die than in battle?

My eyes riveted to an empty space in the dagger display.

A dark-haired man with a long black coat and a badge on his belt conversed with Jack and Mira. The couple talked with wide arm gestures. If I'd listened, I could've caught the gist. But I was lost in the past, numb.

Then I heard Jack say my name. "She's over there, the niece."

I jerked to attention and glanced up. My boss pointed at me. Had he accused me of something?

The dark-haired gentleman about my age approached. "Sandi Jones?"

"Yes, sir."

"I'm Detective James Killian." He moved his coat aside to show his badge. "I'm sorry for your loss."

My lip quivered. "Thank you."

"Mind if I ask a few questions?" He sat in a chair beside mine and pulled out a tablet.

"Not at all."

He asked the perfunctory questions of my address and phone number which I answered.

"Did your uncle have any enemies?"

I blew out a breath. "None that I know of." I repositioned in my chair to face the detective. "How did he die?"

"A knife wound."

"Oh." My hand trembled and moved to my chin. I couldn't imagine. Didn't want to imagine. But still, I wanted to see the crime scene.

"When did you see him last?"

"About a month ago. I came to his Christmas party for the staff."

"Who attended?"

"Everyone in the room. Mira Black, his clerk secretary, along with my boss Jack Hackathorn. The groundskeepers, Gwen and Ron Smith. The gardener, Ryan Brown. And the kitchen staff, Mrs. Moon and...sorry, I can't remember the other woman's name."

"That's okay. We'll get it. How'd the party go? Anything negative stand out?"

I shook my head. "No." *Wait.* "But my uncle pulled me aside and told me that his health had failed him. When I asked about it, he wouldn't tell me anymore." My lip quivered again.

"And the last time you spoke to him?"

"Two days ago."

His brow lifted. "You called him?"

"He called me."

"What did you talk about?"

"He asked about my classes. I'm in my second year."

"Oh? What for?"

"Criminal Justice."

"Interesting." He blinked.

"Yes, I've always wanted to be a PI."

"What else did you talk about?"

"He asked about my book club. If I still went. If I enjoyed it." I drew in a shaky breath. "And, he said someone had embezzled money from his foundation."

The detective's eyes widened as he typed. "Did he say who?"

"Well, only one person handles it."

"Mira Black?"

I nodded.

"Had he reported it to the police?"

"I don't know."

"Well, there's a place to start. Do you know anything about his will?"

"A large portion goes to the foundation. Then me and the staff."

"His employees?"

"Yes. He felt obligated in a way. I don't know how else to explain it."

"Where were you yesterday evening between 5:00 and 7:00 pm.?"

"At my book club." Thoughts of my uncle asking about it flooded my mind. Tears welled in my eyes. "Is there any way I can see him? Did he suffer?"

Detective Killian studied my expression. I must've looked like a forlorn wreck.

"Because of your background, I'll take you to the room." He dropped his voice and infused it with care. "I want to prepare you for the scene. It's not as bad as you might think. The knife punctured the back of his chair. The blow stopped his heart."

"The back of his chair? How odd."

"Yes." He stood and motioned for me to follow.

It felt as though every eye watched us walk to the room. He pushed the door open. We slipped inside. My uncle's expression held every ounce of bravery and peace it could hold. I couldn't see much blood, which would be due to the heart stopping on impact.

The dagger handle held fast in place. The handguard rested against the back of the chair. The steel grip and pommel had no visible marks.

"It's one of the Rondel daggers. From my uncle's display. It's one of his favorites." My legs turned weak. "I need to go and sit down."

"Of course."

The detective accompanied me. I dropped once again onto the chair I'd first occupied.

"Stay a few more minutes. I may have more questions."

I nodded. Some PI I would make. Could I even walk to my car?

Yesterday's conversation about Mira's car hit me over the head. Jack had to pick her up since her car wouldn't start. That placed them both at the scene of the crime between five and seven o'clock. *Oh, boy.* But no doubt the detective had already placed them there.

Time ticked by. Nausea threatened. Jack and Mira strolled toward me.

"What's the deal?" my boss asked.

"I'm sorry?" I had no idea what he meant.

"Why'd he take you back there?" He jerked his head toward the office door.

I shrugged, not in the mood to reward his pettiness.

Mira crossed her arms and frowned. "It's just like Sandi to get preferential treatment."

"He's my uncle." I reminded them again.

The detective hurried toward us. "Please, I still have more questions. Could you two wait at the other side of the room? I'll be with you soon."

Mira clicked her tongue in protest, but she and

Jack made their way to the indicated space.

"What did you tell them?" Killian asked.

"Nothing."

"Good. Keep it that way." He touched my shoulder, then strode away. I rolled forward with my elbows on my knees. Head in hands. I wanted to go home.

Mrs. Moon served coffee and fresh chocolate muffins. I couldn't eat, but the coffee helped. One by one, the staff neared and offered their condolences to me.

Killian returned. "We checked with the department. Your uncle didn't report the theft."

"Hmm. Not like him at all."

"May we have authorization to check your phone records?"

"Of course."

He held out his tablet. I signed off.

"Here's my card if you need to get in touch." He handed me his business card. "Thank you, Ms. Jones. You're free to leave."

"Sandi."

He dipped his head and walked toward Mira and Jack. As I stood and turned to leave, I glanced once more at Uncle Drew's collection. Why had the killer chosen my uncle's favorite dagger? I sighed and bit back tears.

Killian's voice drifted from across the room. "Will you two accompany me to the station?"

"I can't believe it," Mira whined.

Jack shushed her. Then, of all things, he called out to me. "Sandi, I expect you to go straight to the office."

I looked him in the eye. "I quit."

His jaw dropped. "What?"

"She said, 'I quit,'" Killian said with a faint smile.

I turned and left the manor.

****

Eight days passed. I focused on my classes and everyday apartment life. Somehow, I'd planned the funeral and had survived the actual day.

Another morning arrived. As I drank my coffee, thoughts nagged me like broken threads in fine cloth.

Uncle Drew had poor health.

Mira embezzled money.

He didn't call the police.

His favorite dagger killed him. The weapon pierced the chair. Awkward, yet, aimed for the best result.

I gasped as a terrible theory came to mind. But would Uncle Drew do such a thing? He knew he was at death's door. He picked up his favorite dagger and plunged it into the chair, so the point didn't break through the front. He sat down, then pushed the desk chair backward with all his might. The chair dashed against the stone wall. The dagger's pommel hit the hard surface behind him and thrust the blade forward. The chair rebounded and rolled away from the wall. In his mind, he'd died in battle. The dreaded enemy wounded him from behind. A stab in the back.

And who would be suspected? Mira. Payment for her crime against him.

Oh, my goodness. The book club. He'd checked to make sure I'd have an alibi if I were questioned.

Uncle Drew. Would you devise such a scheme?

He wouldn't let an innocent person be charged with murder. But how like him to let Mira stew for a while with a possible murder charge.

 Had he counted on me to figure out the puzzle? If that were the case, he would've left me a note.

****

Days passed. I couldn't find any note. Had I missed a hiding place my uncle thought I knew?

What if Mira and Jack were innocent? I couldn't keep my theory to myself much longer.

As on every other day, I plodded to the mailbox. A strange envelope from a lawyer's office lay on top of junk mail. Now what?

I ripped it open and skimmed the lawyer's letter. He apologized for his tardiness. He'd been out of the country. Please find the enclosed letter from Drew Yetter to be mailed in the event of his death.

With shaky hands, I carried his letter addressed to me. Once inside my apartment, I sat at the kitchen table, opened it, and read. The letter was dated several days before we'd last talked on the phone.

Dear Sandi,

I hope this letter finds you well· I hate to burden you with this, but if I haven't died of natural causes you'll need this information· I've played the part of a deaf and dull-witted man in the presence of two culprits· They've become bold, and I suspect their plan· Will they go through with it? I don't know· I've discovered that Mira Black has stolen money over a two-year period· She and Jack Hackathorn have reached a tidy sum and are worried I'm not as feeble-minded as I've appeared· It's odd that they asked me which of my daggers is my favorite· Will it be their weapon of choice?

If this is the case, don't be sad for me· Remember I've always wanted to die in battle·

Fight the good fight and keep the faith!

I know your private investigator abilities are much needed in this world.

Love,

Uncle Drew

The letter drifted to the table. It had been Mira and Jack all along. They knew how my mind operated because I'd worked with Jack for two years. He would explain how Uncle Drew committed suicide. And I'd agree with him!

They'd assumed any question about their embezzlement died with my uncle.

Their plan couldn't work now.

I picked up the letter, held it close to my heart, and took comfort in his words.

As minutes ticked by, I worried. How could I know the truth beyond any doubt? I put a call through to Killian. Within the hour, he stood at my apartment door. I welcomed him in and poured him coffee. He sat at the table and read the letter as I had a moment before.

"Hmm." He set the paper down and glanced at me.

"I'm concerned about a couple of things."

"What are they?"

"Why didn't my uncle report the theft?"

"Ah. I have an answer for that. According to Mrs. Moon, the landline went out after your uncle had called you on the twenty-fifth. She reported the downed line and offered her cell phone, but he refused."

"That sounds like him."

"The technician didn't come until after he passed." His voice turned grim.

"Why had the phone gone out?"

"The serviceman said it was a combination of high winds and an old line. But I suspect it had been tampered with."

"And about Mira's car. Had it been tampered with also?"

"Nothing wrong with it. Of course, she claimed it wouldn't start. Does that help?"

"Well, part of me worries Uncle Drew framed Mira and Jack for his death. What if his illness…"

"Put your mind to rest. They're both guilty. However, they tried to create doubt by claiming it an elaborate suicide."

"How do you know they did it for sure?"

"We found a botched suicide note Mira forged, half-burned in her fireplace. And this morning, they ratted each other out. Both played the victim card."

I sighed with relief. "Thank you, Detective Killian. I appreciate it more than words can say."

"You're welcome. And please, call me Jim."

Apocalyptic Adventure

A Matter of Minutes

Elizabethtown, Kentucky, June 6, 1999, 1:34 p.m.

Special Agent Jessica Stark hefted her laptop onto the table and opened her email. "*Shoot!*" She slammed her right hand on the wooden surface.

"Don't tell me." Her handsome partner Special Agent Max Boggs clenched his jaw.

She focused on his gray eyes, then blew out a breath, sending a few strands of her red hair into flight.

"It didn't go through, did it?" he asked.

"No, someone deleted it, Max! Our boss needs this information. It's a matter of national security." She lifted a weary hand. "What are we going to do?"

"The only thing we can do. Take the photos and specimens directly to Rittman."

"What if he's a mole?"

Max gripped her shoulder. "I trust our boss. Rittman's the epitome of loyalty. The perpetrator is an outsider."

"I hope you're right."

"We're due back at headquarters in two days. Let's arrive unannounced tomorrow."

"The element of surprise?"

"It's precious little, but it's all we have."

"Oh, man." Jessica stood and paced in her dingy dark-yellow motel room. Random stains covered the shag carpet which she tried to avoid. "We need a backup plan." She lowered her voice. "We need to hide hard copies of our information and at least half of the specimens."

"Okay, let's take a deep breath and look over what we have."

Max pulled out printed photos and typewritten events from his briefcase while Jessica grabbed a black duffle and withdrew five plastic evidence bags filled with samples.

She touched the photos with timestamps. "Once anyone sees this, there's no denying…"

"Agreed." Max rubbed his chin in a thoughtful manner, then studied the walls of the room. He squatted by the desk. "Here. The air vent."

She pressed her lips together. "Let's keep looking."

He nodded and inched his way to the closet.

At the bedframe, she studied the headboard. Could they tape the evidence on the hidden side? Too risky. Her glance took in the carpet, and she dropped to her knees. She touched a tear in the cheap carpet beside a cigarette burn mark.

"Max."

He hastened to her. His line of vision tracked where she pointed. "What about here?" she whispered.

His brow furrowed, then relaxed. His eyes brightened. He pulled out a pocket knife from his pocket and cut a slit parallel to the baseboard underneath the bed. He slipped the photos underneath the carpeting.

"Perfect," she said.

"Yeah, can't even tell."

"What about the specimens?"

He glanced at the air vent.

She gave a brief nod.

After they completed the task, Max headed to the door. "Let's get two hours of sleep before we go."

"Terrific." She waved as he stepped outside to go to his room.

Jessica needed sleep and a couple of hours wouldn't be enough. They'd already driven eight hours from Flippin, Arkansas. Who'd name their hometown that? She squinted her eyes. Probably Max's ancestors.

She slipped under the sheet and heaved a sigh.

Sleep!

After several minutes, she gave up and sat at the table. *Dear, God,* could this really be happening?

Six days ago, Max had received a call from a distant cousin that had set the whole investigation in motion. Of course, her partner always chomped at the bit to study any unexplained phenomena.

Four days ago, they'd arrived in Flippin. They'd interviewed the cousin, Ronny Sacksteder. And even Max had thought the whole mess improbable.

Ronny had said the *takeover* had happened when he'd first noticed a change in a grocery clerk named Marie. She'd always been an empathetic soul, talkative, and carefree, then one day she wasn't. Next to change was her husband, Frank, the town deputy. Then the postal clerks. Each had taken on a different personality, an inner darkness, a controlling, inquisitive nature.

Jessica and Max had posed as a married couple and checked out the town. True, the people designated by Ronnie had a reserved cautious air about them. No smiles graced their lips. No light shone in their eyes.

"Has someone tainted the water? Or perhaps an occurrence in nature is to blame?" she'd posed the questions to Max.

His theories showed a more insidious answer. She'd stopped herself from rolling her eyes.

How tragic that he'd been right.

Jessica picked up a photograph and studied it. Prickles of dread crept up her back.

After the interview, they'd checked out the neighborhoods. Finding nothing, they explored the backroads. An eerie quiet had descended over the area. No bugs in the air. No birds singing. No rodents or wildlife.

Scattered in two field plots, an unusual plant grew with razor-sharp points and short furry tendrils. Unthinking, she'd reached out to touch it, but Max had grabbed her hand. He'd saved her.

Later that night, they'd found one of the town drunks dead and decomposing behind the bar in a bed of the alien plants. Against better judgment, they'd sought out the sheriff. But when they'd returned, the body was gone and a replacement of the man drank in the bar.

The sheriff had demanded an answer for the wild goose chase.

Well, they'd been mistaken.

Wrong.

Max had taken photos of the corpse.

She held the date-stamped photo of 6-3-99 11:34 p.m. and compared it with the next photo of the living man stamped 6-4-99 1:03 a.m. Of course, in a court of law, the authenticity of the photos could be questioned. She, Max, and Rittman knew otherwise. Their boss just needed solid proof to proceed.

Before heading back to DC, Max wanted to

check out another surrounding area close to town. She'd agreed. They'd parked their rental on a dirt road near an overlook and set out on foot. A glint from an object down below had caught Max's eye. They'd climbed down the steep embankment.

That's when they'd found the unusual object. A smooth triangular metal piece about the size of Max's hand. He'd tried to lift it. He'd dug around it to get a better grip. The object dropped farther into the hard-packed rocky soil as if it weighed hundreds of pounds or was greatly influenced by the earth's gravitational pull.

Max had said, "Now do you believe?"

She'd given a solemn nod. Alien life. On earth.

Jessica touched the picture of the metal object. How strange, how foreign.

Minutes passed.

"Let's go," Max said as he touched her arm.

Her eyes blinked open. She'd fallen asleep at the table, and her neck ached.

They packed the car and drove. Night turned into day. Ten hours later, they stepped into Rittman's office as Jessica smoothed her hair.

She and Max sat by a desk opposite their boss.

"Well, where is it?" Rittman asked.

Max placed his black briefcase on his lap and opened it. His jaw dropped. "No."

"What is it?" she asked, her insides turned cold.

"The photos, the plant specimens—they're

gone."

"How can that be?" She leaned to peer in the empty case. "Your camera. Show him the pictures from there."

Rittman cleared his throat. His well-known impatient tic.

Max abandoned the briefcase and grabbed his camera. He tried to scroll through images. The FBI-certified camera dropped to his lap.

"It's been wiped clean." Max took in a shuddered breath. "Check your laptop."

She pulled the machine out of her bag and flipped it open. A blue screen lit. All icons and folders were gone. Vanished. She covered her face in disbelief. Who had done this? How could they fight against an unseen enemy? And their hidden evidence in the motel was no good if they couldn't retrieve it and bring it to DC.

Her hand dropped. "How...how did this happen?" Her voice shook.

"What time do you have?" Max asked.

What? What did that have to do with anything? She glanced at her watch. "Eleven thirty-four."

He held up his hand, showing his wristwatch. "That's what I have." He pointed. "That's the time your computer has."

"Why is that significant?" she whispered.

His eyes lifted to the wall clock behind Rittman's head. Eleven forty-four.

"Okay. I've heard and seen enough. Come back when you have something." Rittman motioned to the door.

She and Max stood as he pulled out his phone. He pushed a number. Outside the office, he held it so both could hear. "The current time is eleven forty-five."

Jessica looked at her watch. "Eleven *thirty-five*?"

"That's right." Max pulled her farther away from Rittman's door. "We're missing ten minutes. That's when everything was taken." His eyes locked with hers. "Missing time, Jessica! We were abducted. Our evidence was taken."

"But when?"

He shrugged. "Could've been any time we were on the road."

Her muscles turned weak. She leaned against the wall. "What kind of technology would it take to pull that off?"

Max tilted his head as if he couldn't believe her question. "I think you know the answer to that."

Believe Me

"Believe me, it's good to get this out of the way," my handsome sandy-haired husband said.

I wasn't so sure and teased Brent with a stink-eye expression as I slumped farther into the Department of Motor Vehicles' plastic chair.

He did a double-take at my squinted eyes and broke out into a gorgeous smile, then chuckled. "Look, we're at the mall anyway." He glanced at the bag I held, containing my maternity dress purchase. "We can kill two birds with one stone."

The cliché rattled through my mind. "Kill? Why kill?" I frowned. "As a new vet in Fox Falls, should you be saying things like that?"

He shrugged. "It's just an expression." His blue eyes the epitome of innocence. "Kinsley, what's up?

Is everything okay?"

"Why?"

Ding! The number twenty lit up. I checked the tag in my hand. Number twenty-three, I sighed.

"You seem, well, not like yourself," he said diplomatically. "You're sassier than usual. You're still okay with moving back, aren't you?"

I contemplated my answer. The small town in Virginia was beautiful. Only a short drive to his parents' house in DC. But she and Brent had moved away from her parents in order to offer help to his. *Alzheimer's.* Truly devastating for his mom and even more so to his dad. He hated to see her lose her mental capabilities.

Our eyes locked, and I squeezed his hand. "Of course."

Ding! I glanced at the lit sign. Number twenty-one.

We gazed out the window into the twilight. Minutes ticked by.

A pink flash lit up the sky, then disappeared as fast as it came. Were my eyes playing tricks on me?

"Did you see that?" I asked.

Eyes wide, Brent nodded.

A loud boom sounded, followed by a rumble. The little DMV attached to the Ivy Mall shook. The people awaiting their turns gasped. Some swore. Several young men stood and stepped toward the window. A couple rushed outside.

I clutched Brent's arm. "What was that? What happened?"

He put his arm around me. "I don't know. Nothing good."

Ding! Number twenty-two.

We collectively pulled out our phones.

"Don't bother," said a classy woman with a distinct accent. "Service is out."

I loved her cheerful yellow African print dress and head wrap, but it didn't soften the shock. Was it true?

"What?" My husband's jaw dropped. "Seriously?"

The woman in yellow held up her phone, showing us the black screen. A retired couple next to her also showed us their dark screens.

I fidgeted in my chair. "Brent, I don't like this."

"What's that?" an uptight man exclaimed. He was the most distinguished man in the room with an impeccable gray suit, white shirt, and red tie. His dark hair and goatee even more impressive with touches of gray. But he gave off vibes of an arrogant jerk. He stepped closer to see out the windows. "It looks hazy."

The evening air appeared dense. A grayish-pink. The younger couple who had left in a hurry returned, coughing. They dropped into chairs located by the door. "Don't go out there," the guy said between dry coughs.

"Okay." The man in the suit strung out the word in an irritated fashion.

I tentatively tried to test the air with my next intake of breath. A hint of sulfur? Or was it my imagination?

An odd vapor neared and swirled outside against the glass door and windows.

"Oh, no," I said as I caught a glimpse of a gray-bearded man in the parking lot. He took short steps and coughed as he staggered between vehicles. Would he make it to the door?

"I should go help him." Brent moved in his chair to stand.

I grabbed his arm. "No," I pleaded, almost ashamed of myself. "We don't know what that stuff is."

"I have to."

I lost grip of his arm, and he headed to the door in long strides. Halfway to the door, I caught up with him and clung to his arm. "If you go, I'll go too."

He hesitated and glanced at my small baby bump. "You can't."

"I'm worried for the guy outside too. But please don't go."

We thought we only spoke to each other, but everyone in the waiting area had their attention focused on us.

The couple seated by the door still coughed. "Don't do it," the guy said. He looked behind his shoulder out the window. "It's much worse out there now."

Brent sighed sadly and ran a hand over his face. We couldn't stop looking at the gray-bearded man. I pulled my husband back to our seats.

"Internet's down," said a large woman behind the counter. Her line of vision reached the window and beyond. Her face paled. She sat heavily in a chair as her coworker talked to her.

The man in the suit lifted his hands. "Well, that figures. I guess I'll have to come back later."

Another clerk spoke up. "We can process your requests manually on paper."

The distinguished man made a shushing noise and grumbled under his breath. He headed to the hall that linked the office to the main mall. His expensive shoes clicked on the cheap linoleum tile as he strode away. Everyone else stayed seated. What else could we do to pass time? I was sure no one wanted to go to their car. The parking lot had become a surreal wasteland. A strange pinkish film covered the vehicles. We'd parked at the far end of the mall. Had the haze reached our car?

I returned my attention to Brent.

His eyes widened. "Look, he's almost made it."

Ding! Number twenty-three.

"That's us," I said.

We stood.

The poor soul outside took a step onto the

sidewalk and headed for the window instead of the door.

If he came inside, the tainted air would waft in. The man continued to cough. Dark spittle dripped from his mouth. Shocked, I prayed for his safety. Saddened, I hadn't done so right away. *Please, help him. Protect us.*

Brent gritted his teeth. He took a step. "I have to help him."

"Please don't. He's going to make it."

A young female clerk waved at us. "I can help you here."

Reluctantly, Brent complied with a sigh. We sat at her station. The girl couldn't have been more than nineteen.

"It's insane out there. Hope it clears up soon."

"Yeah." My husband's one-syllable response said it all. The disaster wasn't likely to clear up anytime soon.

"You're here to pick up your license plate?"

Brent nodded.

"Fill out this information." She handed him a paper. "I'll be right back with your plate.

I turned and glanced outside. The bearded man ran his fingers along the window as if it were the entrance.

Brent quickly filled out the paperwork, and we signed our names.

The girl returned and placed the license on the

table. "Science fiction fanatic, are you?"

"Yes, but—"

In a conspiratorial tone, the girl said, "Since you're new here, we're supposed to verify the information by going outside to see your car's odometer and FEIN. But I'll let that pass, under the circumstances." She stared out the window. "Oh, dear."

Brent and I turned and looked. The gray-bearded man still lingered in the haze. He thumped his head against the window which was six feet away from us. He'd worked his way down the windows away from the entrance. Dark spittle still dripped from the man's mouth. And of all things, his mouth opened and closed over and over again. The spittle changed to a white foam and oozed out of his mouth. The jerking motions turned into lunging snapping bites as his eyes focused on us. How odd.

"I can't believe it," Brent said with astonishment. He turned to the girl urgently. "We have to lock the door. Who has the key?"

She stared at Brent in disbelief.

He lifted his voice to the other clerks and repeated, "We must lock the door. Where is the key? You've got to trust me on this." Brent stood and pointed to the man. "He's showing advanced signs of rabies. I've never seen it progress so rapidly."

Shocked murmurs reverberated around them.

Frozen in place, the clerks stared wide-eyed.

"Now! We need the key now! He's contagious. With a rapidly progressing disease!"

A middle-aged blonde reached into a desk drawer and pulled out a key. Brent rushed toward her and hastily held out a hand for the key, but she folded it into her fist.

"Please give me the key. It's not safe."

The blonde rolled her eyes and strode toward the door. "I'll do it."

Brent followed her, clearly upset. I grabbed the license plate and hurried after him. He held out an arm. "Stay here."

I followed him.

The blonde reached the door. Brent stopped, so I wouldn't get any nearer to the danger.

The sick man must've seen us rush to the entry. In an attempt to get closer to us, he neared the door. He closed his mouth and wiped his face with a sleeve, then stood as if calmly waiting for a bus.

The woman lifted the key to the lock. She tilted her head, and her shoulders slumped. "Why, there's nothing wrong with him."

Good grief. Was the woman blind? His shirt was sopping wet with dark liquid. While she hesitated, the man pushed the door. She stumbled aside. His head and shoulders slid through. He bit her uplifted hand that held the key.

The woman screamed, her eyes riveted on her bleeding fingers. The key dropped to the floor.

Brent sprang at the door and pushed it shut, hitting the man who teetered backward and thrust a hand at the doorframe. Brent continued to shove the door. I lunged for the key, knocking the blonde clerk off balance.

I blinked.

The door was shut. I jabbed the key in the lock and turned it. The bolt locked in place. My body trembled. I heaved a sigh of relief.

Brent put his arm around me and steadied me. "Good job," he said softly.

I gazed at the foolish clerk who sat on the floor and held her injured hand.

"I can't believe he bit me."

I was the one to roll my eyes now.

"You'll need to get medical attention as soon as it's possible." Brent helped the woman to her feet and held her elbow until she was seated.

"Um," I said as I happened to see something on the floor by the locked door.

Brent caught my line of vision and studied the object with a stunned expression. The man's hand lay on the floor. No blood or liquid surrounded the wrist as if it'd been dead for a long time.

I glanced up. The rabid man toddled toward the door, lifting his stump.

"I think it's worse than rabies," I whispered. "What could it be? Rabies with a side of leprosy?"

Brent placed a hand on his hip and blew out a

breath. I knew what he was thinking. *Zombie apocalypse.*

When I looked around the room to see how everyone had taken the new development, the office had nearly emptied. The black woman in yellow beckoned us to leave with her. The retired couple headed to the narrow hallway leading to the mall.

"We gotta get out of here," one of the young men said to the others.

They hastily agreed.

The young couple seated by the door started to open and close their mouths.

"Brent!" I pointed to them.

His hair almost stood on end. He reached to help the blonde clerk, but her eyes tracked his arm as if she would bite.

I picked up the license plate from the floor and slipped it into my shopping bag. We followed the older couple and the woman in yellow to the mall.

The last uncontaminated ones out, we heaved a sigh of relief as we exited the DMV door.

"Wait. Do you still have the key?"

Did I? I touched my pants pocket. I had inadvertently slipped it there. I pulled it out. Could we find help for those left behind? I swallowed hard. A grisly death seemed too certain. Brent grasped the key and locked the door. Again, relief lightened my shoulders, but it was short-lived as I remembered the other main entrances.

Our friends from the DMV had hastened in different directions. I hoped they had some form of escape and would warn others. Our car waited at the other end of the mall. Worrisome, since it was far away, yet the massive buildings somewhat shielded the parking lot. Hopefully, the full brunt of the haze hadn't reached there yet.

Brent locked eyes with me, and we took off in a jog. A shiver enveloped me as I saw the distinguished man from the DMV clutch his arm as he teetered into a wall. Three infected women swarmed him for another bite. Shoppers, eerily dusted in grayish-pink, coughed as they sat on benches or leaned against walls.

"We don't have a chance, Brent."

"There's always a chance," he said with conviction.

"Did you notice which direction the flash of light came from?

His eyes shot to mine. Drowning realization hit his face. "DC," he said softly. "*Dear, God, no.*"

"Is it an attack? Chemical warfare?"

"No way to know. We've got to get to the car."

Brent clutched my hand as we sprinted through the mall, helpless to come to anyone's aid. Distant cries echoed from stores and other hallways. Anyone we neared, Brent warned about the contamination.

At last, we reached the endcap department store, Trumbles. We raced to the escalator to get to the lower level. It'd stopped working. Not a good sign. We descended, our feet slamming against metal. When we reached the last step, the lights winked out.

Gasps of dismay sounded in the store. Brent squeezed my hand. "It might be a good thing. People can hide or try to escape to their cars. That is if the air is any better at this end."

We reached the shoe department and the exit. I couldn't determine the air quality in the darkening sky. But vehicles didn't appear to have any of the insidious film covering them. I pushed on the first set of glass doors.

"Wait." Brent touched my arm. "Give me the dress."

"What?" I'm sure I looked at him as if he'd lost his mind and handed it to him.

"We'll use it to cover our mouths and noses. It will offer some protection." He pulled out a pocket knife and cut, then tore the pretty rose-colored dress in half lengthwise.

It made me sick at heart, but it wasn't as devastating as the impending plague. He carefully wrapped the material around me, then did the same for himself.

"Do you have a paper and pen?" he asked.

"I think so."

I searched my purse and pulled out the items. He quickly scrawled on the lined notecard. *Don't breathe the air. Cover your nose and mouth.* He pulled back a corner of a sticky decal on the door and stuck the note to it.

He winced. "I hope that helps."

I touched his shoulder.

"Ready?" he asked.

I nodded.

We plunged into the evening air. An odd sulfur odor reached my nostrils. We dashed to our white SUV. I tapped the door. No residue.

I hopped in. My husband slid behind the wheel. Would the car start?

He turned the key. The engine turned over. I breathed a prayer of thanks. "Where are we going?"

"Anywhere that's far away from the haze."

I tossed the bag with the license plate onto the backseat. Brent saw the motion and grimaced.

"Still like the vanity plate?" I asked.

He frowned wearily and hit the gas.

Moments later, we headed west. I checked my phone, still nothing. Thankfully, most of the traffic sped in the same direction. Brent flashed high-beam lights on any cars heading east as a warning. Soon, cars ahead of us and behind us also shined warnings to the oncoming traffic.

Brent removed his makeshift mask, and I did the same. Would we need them again? I shuddered. What if DC wasn't the only city to receive a toxic blast?

The whirring sound of the tires on the road made

me drowsy despite the horror we had witnessed.

The next thing I knew, my eyes opened.

I was in bed. Our bed. My husband lay beside me. I put a hand on his back to wake him. What a horrible dream I'd had. Would I ever get over it? It had to be because of Brent's word choice for our license plate. I couldn't blame him. He was a kid at heart. He loved scary stories. He loved to joke around.

But he also wanted to get people to think.

"Brent, wake up," I said.

He stirred. Something was off. Was he sick?

"Wake up," I repeated and gently shook his shoulder.

He mumbled something. He breathed evenly in a deep slumber.

It was only a dream.

We are safe, I told myself.

I relaxed.

"Wake up." My husband's voice seemed to call from far away. *Wake up?* I'd been trying to get him to wake up.

A hand shook my shoulder. My eyes flew open. I gulped in air.

Oh, no. Prickles of fear tingled over my face and down my back. We were in the car, racing at breakneck speed.

"Grab the material, cover your nose and mouth," my husband yelled.

I quickly did as he said, then covered him as he

drove.

Pinkish wisps swirled on the road. I could think of nothing but the license plate on the backseat.

R M A G D N

Armageddon.

About the Author

Jackie Zack loves to read and grew up reading Phyllis A. Whitney, Victoria Holt, Agatha Christie, and many others. A member of American Christian Fiction Writers, Jackie has spent many years studying the craft of writing. Her light-hearted novels include a mix of romance, comedy, and suspense with Christian characters. She loves serving up her special blend of entertainment and hopes it will bring much enjoyment to the reader. Among her books are *An Irish Heart*, *Rafe's Café*, *The Teacup Conspiracy*, and *Ice Lake* – the Katy Russell mystery series. Her books are available at Amazon.

To sign up for Jackie's newsletter, please visit the contact page at jackiezack.wordpress.com. The monthly newsletter will have information about updates, specials, and free ebooks. She'd love to see you there.

Made in the USA
Coppell, TX
22 October 2023

23216684R00052